WITCHES, GHOSTS & Loups-Garous

Other books by Joan Finnigan from Quarry Press

Wintering Over

The Watershed Collection

Legacies, Legends & Lies

Old Scores, New Goals:
The Story of the Ottawa Senators

Finnigan's Guide to the Ottawa Valley

Dancing at the Crossroads

WITCHES, GHOSTS & Loups-Garous

SCARY TALES FROM CANADA'S OTTAWA VALLEY

RETOLD BY

JOAN FINNIGAN

QUARRY PRESS

For my grandchildren Matthew, Caitlin, Iain, Genevieve, Maria, and Maura.

The published gratefully acknowledges the assistance of The Canada Council, the Ministry of Canadian Heritage, the Ontario Arts Council, and the Ontario Publishing Centre.

Cataloguing in Publication Data

Finnigan, Joan, 1925 –
   Witches, Ghosts & Loup-Garous: Scary Tales from Canada's Ottawa Valley

ISBN 1-55082-086-9

   1. Witches, ghosts & loup-garous, Canadian (English) — Ottawa River Valley (Quebec and Ont.). 2. Tales — Ottawa River Valley (Quebec and Ont.). 3. Legends — Ottawa River Valley (Quebec and Ont.). I. Title.

FC2778. G46F46   1993   398.2'5'097138   C93-090517-2
F1054.09F46   1993

All photographs by Joan Finnigan.
Design Consultant: Keith Abraham.
Printed and bound in Canada by Webcom Limited, Toronto, Ontario.

Published by **Quarry Press**, Inc.
P.O. Box 1061, Kingston, Ontario K7L 4Y5.

Contents

The Burial of Bandy Burke
& Other Dark Legends

Preface

BEFORE the arrival of European explorers, the country we now know as Canada was viewed as a mysterious and frightening place, peopled by the imagination with strange mythological creatures. In 1550 when Pierre Desceliers, a Normandy priest, created his map of Eastern Canada, he drew in rampant unicorns, gaggles of ostriches, and pygmies on the warpath armed with bows and darts. But Samuel de Champlain's explorations following 1613 opened the way for geographically correct maps, and by 1700 fairly accurate images of the whole of Eastern North America were available and the Native inhabitants well known.

If the realities of the explorers and map makers dissolved the unicorns, ostriches, and pygmies, the imaginations of the trappers, the settlers, and the shantymen filled the new wildernesses and unpeopled silences with another set of strange and often frightening creatures and spirits like the Witch-Canoe, the Loup-Garou, and the Walker-in-the-Snow. Not surprisingly, many of these legends originated in the Ottawa Valley, settled during the eighteenth and nineteenth centuries by Scottish and Irish immigrants who brought with them the art of storytelling and a fertile imagination. Many of these settlers came to the Ottawa Valley to work in the lumber trade, cutting timber in the bush during the fall and winter while living in shanties, driving the logs down river during the spring and summer. Myriads of ghost stories and scary tales emerged from these lumber camps in Ontario and Quebec. Miles from any other human habitation, isolated in the midst of a vast wilderness, the shanties provided an atmosphere for men's imaginations running wild in the very human attempt to people the emptiness, and for the invention of scary tricks, largely for the amusement of bored and isolated men.

Many of the lumbering-related ghost stories and scary tales I retell in this book came from people I interviewed for my oral histories of the Ottawa Valley — *Some of the Stories I Told You Were True, Laughing All the Way Home, Legacies, Legends & Lies, Tell Me Another*

Story. Generally speaking, these stories came from old shantymen and rivermen themselves, like the McCullough brothers of North Bay, Gordon and Clarence, both of whom had been involved in shantying, as their father before them, and in particular from Edgar Burwash who told me his ancestral story of "The Dripping Seaman." This tale, like many oral legends, has a basis in fact, even though the "facts" have been embellished over the generations. George Usborne, the chief character in the story, was an early lumber baron who conducted business along the St. Lawrence and the Ottawa River. If you go north of Ottawa to Portage-du-Fort today, you can see his large stone storage sheds (now transformed into a summer place) sitting over the Chenaux Falls, the church he built on the hillside, and the burial stone for him and his wife Mary Ogden Seaton in the nave.

When I interviewed the late Emile Bertrand at his kitchen table in Fort Coulonge, Quebec, he told me many great stories. Perhaps the greatest of Bertrand's stories is "The Burial of Bandy Burke," in which he himself, as a very short shantyman, is the main character. Almost all of the stories in this book have been read many times to groups of students, to audiences of teachers, to storytellers gathered at conferences, but "The Burial of Bandy Burke" generally horrifies an older urban audience the most and inspires total disbelief in others. Yet I believe this is a true story which took place in the 1930s in a lumber camp in the wilderness. What modern urban readers have to understand is that a shantyman could not survive his tough life in isolation without ingenuity, inventiveness, and ruthlessness, three characteristics amply displayed in "The Burial of Bandy Burke" as the body is severed and put back together.

Up the Ottawa River, north of the Nation's Capital, Pontiac County in Western Quebec was settled by Scots, English, French, German, Polish, and Irish pioneers, but along Highway 148, also called the Eardley Road, mostly by the superstitious, folklorish Irish. This may account for the richness of the ghost and witch stories throughout the area: the Ghost of Greermount, the Ghost Girl of the Picanoc, the Chichester Ghost, the Ghost Daggs of Elmside, the Witch of Waltham, the Ghosts of the Old Indian Trail, the Ghosts of Ghost Hill near Breckenridge, and, perhaps most famous of all, the Witch Doctors and Witches of Eardley. Somewhere along this one hundred and fifty mile stretch of riverside road running between the mountains and the Ottawa River, high up on the height of land, there exists the remnants of the Old Indian Trail. It is claimed that certain people of special powers can still find traces of this trail with its lookouts spaced along it, used so long ago by the Algonquin tribe to observe the approach of their enemies, the fierce Iroquois, and the European strangers traveling the Ottawa in waves of explorers, missionary-priests, fur traders, lumbermen, and settlers. So among all the Witches of Eardley flying overhead in the shadow of the old mountains and the Ghosts of Ghost Hill moving along the highway, there are also the spirits of the Algonquins on guard on the plateau above the riverfront.

Now Eardley was so richly haunted and so profoundly magical that there is even a story told about an Eardley storyteller named Daly McAra who spooked himself. McAra used to tell stories around his neighbors' kitchen tables by the fire on long winter nights and he used to tell them in such a vivid and convincing manner that his listeners were almost able to see the ghosts, spooks, and witches moving in front of their very eyes. But that was not all. McAra was such an incredible storyteller that he often hypnotized himself with fear and terror and was too afraid to go home alone at night along Highway 148 and up Ghost Hill!

Canada is such a young country and so close chronologically to the origins of its folk tales, legends, and myths that it is still possible for us to document these through people living today or those who have had the stories passed down for only a generation or two. For instance, I am certain, if you wished verification for the tale of "The Raising of the Dead at Waltham," you could find people who were there in the 1920s or descendants who have had the story passed down to them. You should still be able to find in Vinton, Quebec, Sloans who can document the exhuming of John Sloan's wife, recounted in the story of "The Ghost of John Sloan's Wife."

Some of the other stories in *Witches, Ghosts & Loups-Garous,* like "The Spell of the Enchanted Well," "The Legend of Haunted Lake," and "The Return of the Dead," are retold from the tales of old-timers published in the Ottawa newspapers of the 1930s. And some stories, like "The Wolves of Malakoff," "The Man with the Rabbit's Eye," and "The Specter of Widow Holly," grew from a germ of an idea planted in the author's imagination. The photographs of spooky landscapes and haunted houses illustrating the stories have been shot while traveling the Ottawa Valley in search of ghost stories, though none of my photographs of witches or loups-garous turned out.

The Wolves of Malakoff

& Other Haunting Tales

The Wolves
of Malakoff

THIS is a story about John Goth of Malakoff, one of the most famous settlers of Canada who was living in the Ottawa Valley in 1892 when all the wolves left Torbolton Township.

Now one of the reasons John Goth of Malakoff was famous was because he could cut and split three cords of wood a day, and that was near record, if not *the* record. He was also famous because on his ninetieth birthday, when all his family and neighbors and clans were gathered at Malakoff for his birthday party, he climbed a split-rail fence and step-danced on top of the fence-post. When he was ninety-four, he was asked on his birthday if he could dance on the fence-post again for his birthday celebrations.

"Well, now," said John Goth of Malakoff. "By jiggers, I think I can. But this time I might need a little ladder to help me up."

Now back in the early days in the Ottawa Valley the countryside everywhere was thick with bears and wolves. Even back then, wise men knew how smart the animals were. And especially the wolves. And John Goth of Malakoff was certainly old enough to be wise.

Now John Goth of Malakoff had two fine big farm collies named Blackie and Whitey. Blackie was named Blackie because she had more black than white on her and Whitey was named Whitey because he had more white than black on him. Blackie and Whitey were very very good guard dogs. They could hear a toad hop-hopping about under the kitchen stoop trying to catch a blue bottle fly. They could hear a wailing banshee ten miles away. They could hear a weasel slipping into the henhouse to steal a chicken on a moonless night. They could hear the fairies dancing on pumpkins in the garden at Halloween.

Of course, like all good farm collies, Blackie and Whitey slept outside in the wood-shed so they could always be on guard, especially at night. So John Goth of Malakoff was really surprised when, one fall evening just as he was settling his fire for the night in his wood-stove, he heard Blackie and Whitey scratching and whining at the kitchen door.

"Now that's very strange, indeed," said John Goth of Malakoff. "They have never done that before. Something must be wrong . . ."

So he opened the door and in came Blackie and Whitey, crouched low, ears down, so full of fear they crept in under the old couch in the kitchen that John Goth of Malakoff used for his after-lunch nap.

Just as the dogs hid under the kitchen couch, through the open doorway John Goth of Malakoff heard a great howling of wolves starting up near the barns, a great howling of wolves the like of which John Goth had never heard before in all his livelong life. He went upstairs and awakened Malcolm Hamilton, his hired man.

"Get dressed, Malcolm," said John Goth of Malakoff, "and load your gun. We are being invaded, serenaded by an army of wolves on the howl, on the prowl, on the prowl-howl, on the howl-prowl . . ."

And John Goth of Malakoff quickly jumped out of his nightgown and into his work clothes. He was in such haste he almost got into his Sunday clothes by mistake. Then John Goth of Malakoff and his hired man, Malcolm Hamilton, shaking at the hands and knees, lit two lanterns, took two guns, opened the kitchen door, and headed towards the barns.

The howling of the wolves was like nothing they had ever heard on earth before, or even in Malakoff before. As they crossed the barnyard the howling grew louder and louder, and many, many dark forms were seen in the light of the lanterns, dark forms moving with their many many even darker shadows following behind them.

"There must be hundreds of them!" said John Goth of Malakoff to his hired man who could not hear him for the chattering of his teeth.

John Goth of Malakoff fired his gun in the direction of the moving howling mass of wolves. But not a wolf fell. Only the louder and louder cries of the wolves rose in the dark windy night. Then the hired man, Malcolm Hamilton, fired his gun in the direction of the moving howling mass of wolves. But not a wolf fell. Instead, the army of wolves on the run started to move off from the barns to John Goth's far forest of pines. One after another, like wild horses in a stampede, the swift dark forms moved into the woods.

There in John Goth's pinery they gathered together again and there they howled all night long, sometimes all in one voice, sometimes calling out to one another, one by one. And John Goth of Malakoff and his hired man, Malcolm Hamilton, sat in the kitchen by the stove with their lamp lit all night long listening to the wolves in the far forest.

"I have heard the wolves at night call out to one another," said John Goth of Malakoff, "and I know that each one has a different call with different meanings — but I have never heard anything like this before in all my livelong life."

And the hired man replied, "Yes, I have seen packs of wolves in the Shining Tree Country and at the Headwaters of the Ivanhoe, deep into the District of Temiskamingue and at the far-off beginnings of the great Ottawa River. But never have I seen packs of hundreds, running and howling together . . ."

"Yes, something very strange, very weird is going on," said John Goth of Malakoff.

At sunrise the howling of the wolves ceased in John Goth's far forest. The two weary men opened the door and looked out.

Behold! The army of wolves was still gathered in the woods. Three big wolves could be seen standing on a huge fallen log at the edge of the woods. They were looking down into the rest of the pack.

All day long the wolves rested in the woods, silently gathered together as though they were having a council meeting, a pow-wow, and plotting their next move.

With their guns loaded John Goth of Malakoff and his hired man, Malcolm Hamilton, went to the barns and did their daily chores, then carefully secured all the animals inside and returned to the house. At night as soon as the lamps were lit, the army of wolves in the woods began to howl again, a wild loud chorus of wolf cries, enough to send tremors and shakes through any brave man.

It was a moonlit night, and as John Goth of Malakoff and his hired man Malcolm Hamilton looked through the kitchen window, suddenly the wolves ceased their long mournful cries and with one accord began to run, one after another, in their uncounted numbers, out of the far forest and into the moonlight. In uncounted numbers the wolves ran and passed before the eyes of the two men at the window, and disappeared into the moonlight, leaving Malakoff forever.

And not a wolf was ever to be seen again by anyone in the whole of Torbolton Township. Or by John Goth of Malakoff who lived to be one hundred and two and continued to chop and split three cords of wood a day and to dance on top of a fence-post on all his birthdays. But after ninety-four he did need a ladder to climb up. Just a little ladder.

The Loup-Garou of Rocher Fendu

MANY many years ago in the village of Rocher Fendu on the upper Ottawa River, a young man by the name of Joe Thibeau married a young girl by the name of Rosie Holden. One day shortly after they were married, young Joe was setting out early in the morning to fetch a load of straw from a farmer some miles away.

As he was leaving, young Thibeau said to his wife, "Keep your eyes peeled for the return of the load— for you will see a dog driving it."

Of course, Rosie didn't believe Joe. But that night, sure enough, towards dusk as she was peering out of the window of their cabin in the wilderness, Rosie saw the horses and load coming back down the road. And perched on top of the load was a huge dog, sitting on its haunches and holding the reins in its paws!

Terrified at the sight, Rosie grabbed a stout stick and struck the animal a resounding blow across the back. Instantly the dog vanished and her young husband stood before her with a devilish grin on his face.

"See, Rosie," he laughed. "I told you so!"

There and then the young wife prepared to pack her belongings and leave the house. The priest and her parents came to her and told her she could not go.

"You cannot leave your husband!" they cried. "It is against the law of the land, the law of the church, and the law of God!"

"I have married the Devil," Rosie said. "But I am certainly not going to live with him any longer."

And she left the house, never to return again.

ANOTHER time, many years ago up in the Nickabeau on McGillvray Lake, a man named Willie Nephin and his wife Nonnie, in the dead of winter just about dusk, heard a wolf howling on the lake, running around and howling on the lake like a banshee.

Now the Nephins lived in a log house in the wilderness by the side of the lake where they trapped and fished and hunted. So Willie Nephin took his gun off the wall and walked down to the shore. He got a clear shot at the wolf, fired, and then watched as the wolf ran off into a clump of big cedars.

It was too late in the evening for Willie to track the wolf, which he thought he likely killed but certainly knew he had wounded.

"Never mind," he said to his wife. "I'll track him in the morning. He can't get far."

There was a bounty on wolves in those days, about ten dollars, and that was a lot of money back then.

"I'll go with you," his wife said to him. "Just to make sure."

So early the next morning as soon as it was light, Willie and Nonnie set off to track the wounded wolf, finish it off, skin it, and get the money for the bounty on it.

Willie knew exactly where the wolf had gone into the clump of big cedars. When he and his wife got there, sure enough, there was blood on the snow where the wounded wolf had thrashed around.

But the only other marks on the snow were those of a man's footprints walking away into the wilderness.

SOME years later in July, 1880, a young man named Louis Soucier was walking the road from Fort Coulonge to La Passe on the Ottawa River. He had been working for Damase Gervais, helping him with his crop and had gone home to Fort Coulonge for the weekend.

It was a very dark moonless and starless night and Louis was crossing a sandy plain which was skirted by a pine forest. The sandy plain was hard walking and Louis was going along with his head down to make the walking easier. Then something caused him to raise his head. There three feet ahead of him, suddenly looming up out of the dark was a man dressed in black clothes wearing a stiff-collared pure white shirt. But horror of horrors! He had no head!

The hair rose on Louis' own head and he was frozen with fear. He sidestepped to let the headless man pass by. But as quickly as Louis moved, the headless man followed him and stood before him again — only this time a foot closer!

Instinctively Louis struck out at the headless man before him. He then saw blood on the man's white shirt front and there immediately appeared before him the familiar form of one of the best-known men in La Passe.

He was a loup-garou and the drawing of blood from Louis' blow had freed him from a nine year curse!

The man confessed to Louis that he had committed a serious sin years ago by selling his soul to the Devil for money. Every night after that, according to the Devil's decree, he had been forced to walk the roads of La Passe. If, while haunting those roads, he were killed by someone, his soul would go to the Devil. But, if somebody should only injure him and draw his blood, he would be freed from the bargain he had made with the Devil.

The man made Louis Soucier promise never to reveal to anyone his true identity. And Louis Soucier went to his grave without ever telling anyone the real name of the Loup-Garou of La Passe.

The Golden Cave on the Madawaska

MANY years ago the Na-Wa-Kesh family of Algonquin Indians on the Golden Lake Reserve found gold in a cave on the Madawaska River. The exact site of this cave of gold was kept secret for generations in the family until finally only one old Indian woman was left who knew how to get to the Golden Cave. Her name was Neykia.

Many white men of the area had heard rumors of the cache of gold on the Madawaska and, over the years, some of them had tried to follow Neykia whenever she got into her canoe. They would lie in wait all night long and then, at dawn when she slipped down to the water, they would be ready to pursue her at a distance. But Neykia was very wise in the ways of the wilderness; no matter how quiet, how stealthy, how elusive were her pursuers, she always knew at once that she was being followed.

Sometimes, if the white men were slow paddlers, she would set off at top speed and disappear before their very eyes. Sometimes she would thread through the islands of the Madawaska River and lose them. Sometimes she would shoot dangerous rapids which the white men then had to portage around. Sometimes she would beach her canoe and simply disappear like a ghost into the forest. The white men would then find only her empty canoe on shore.

Following Neykia to find the hidden source of the gold, white men were drowned in the Madawaska, sucked down into the white-water rapids, swallowed up by the forest, and never seen again.

But finally two Bertrand brothers from Fort Coulonge on the Quebec side of the Ottawa River decided to follow the gold trail on the Madawaska. Pierre and Louis had spent most of their lives hunting and trapping with the Indians and had learned the art of canoeing from them.

"We know how to keep up with the Indians," boasted Pierre and Louis as they prepared to leave for the Madawaska. "Just you watch us. We will follow Neykia and find the gold."

So loud and boastful were Pierre and Louis that word of their arrival on the Madawaska to find the cave of gold preceded them to Golden Lake. Neykia made them wait in the bush five days before she slipped down to the shore of the Madawaska and got into her canoe. Afterwards, hunters, trappers, and rivermen said that they saw Pierre and Louis in their canoe following Neykia. But the two brothers never returned home to Fort Coulonge.

After several weeks search parties were sent out to try to find the men, or the bodies of the men. On the shore of the Madawaska just above Rogue's Harbour searchers found a fresh grave, a pile of stones with a rough wooden cross erected on it.

When an autopsy was done the body in the grave site was positively identified as that of Pierre Bertrand. But Louis had entirely vanished.

Neykia died a few years later. As far as anybody knows, she took with her to the grave the secret of the site of the cave of gold.

But even to this day white men still search the Madawaska River for the golden cave.

The Spirit of Alice Snowshoes

In many of the Indian tribes of the Ottawa Valley it was the custom to leave behind their old people who could not keep up with the movements and pace of the tribe. The people of the tribe put pitch in the old people's eyes, blindfolded them and left them behind to die because the survival of the tribe was more important than any one single person.

Old Alice Snowshoes, an Algonquin Indian, was left to die on the Eardley Road near Aylmer, Quebec, in front of the Donald McLean house. Mrs. McLean heard Alice Snowshoes moaning outside, brought her into the house, wiped the pitch from her eyes, and nursed her back to health. She lived with the McLeans ever afterwards, helping with the housework, making baskets, moccasins and beaded mitts, acting as midwife and using her knowledge of herbs to help sick people.

In those early days there were no doctors. So Alice Snowshoes traveled the countryside, through blizzards, rain storms, and dark nights to help people who were ill, making her way through the wilderness to the settler's cabin with her medicine bag and her own scant supply of food.

Nobody ever knew how she knew that people were ill and needed her help. She seemed to have some special native instinct that told her help was needed by families isolated and many miles away. And she would travel to them and fall like a ghost from the sky. Without any word or warning, she would just suddenly be there at the bedside of the sick child, or the young mother in labor, or the injured father.

In many log houses all through the Ottawa Valley many an evening prayer was offered for Alice Snowshoes, the good spirit they could always count on, who would never fail them, who appeared always like a ghost out of nowhere.

After helping many generations of sick people, Alice Snowshoes died on Christmas Day, 1874, at the age of one hundred and twenty. Her body was taken to Quyon by members of her tribe and buried somewhere deep in the forest. But the spot of her last resting place has never been revealed to the people she helped so much.

The Legend of Haunted Lake

MANY years ago before the Ottawa tribe had been virtually wiped out by the Iroquois, Chief A-Wah-Noh ruled the Ottawas. They lived on an exquisite little lake in the Ottawa Valley, now on the outskirts of Hull, Quebec. His daughter, the lovely Mah-Nah-Ta, had been selected in her infancy to be the wife of the son of another powerful chief, the fathers hoping that the bond would strengthen their forces in the stand against the powerful and aggressive Iroquois.

As Mah-Nah-Ta grew into maidenhood and became eligible to be married, she failed to fit in with the scheming fathers' political aims, instead falling in love with one of the young braves of her tribe, O-We-Tah by name. On the day of the Feast of Midsummer Moon, O-We-Tah demanded of A-Wah-Noh his daughter's hand in marriage. At the same time he boldly challenged in mortal combat any tribesman who disputed his right to Mah-Nah-Ta as his wife.

Under the laws of his race, A-Wah-Noh could only refuse his consent to the marriage by accepting O-We-Tah's challenge. This he promptly did, placing the young warrior in terrible conflict. A-Wah-Noh was an old man and no match for the young O-We-Tah. To kill his beloved's father meant that they would be parted forever, again according to tribal law. But to refuse the contest meant eternal disgrace. O-We-Tah felt he had no choice but to accept the old man's challenge.

Then before the assembled tribe he outlined his plan for the combat. At midnight each man was to station himself exactly opposite the other on the shores of their lake, armed with whatever weapon he chose. A still hunt for each other was then to begin, only to end at daylight or with the death of one of the opponents. Agreeing on this strategy, the two men left the communal campfire and started for their places on the opposite sides of the lake.

Unbeknownst to the rest of the tribe, Mah-Na-Tah had also left the campfire to try to walk off her anxieties and fears in the deep forest surrounding the little lake. She felt she could not bear the suspense of the long night in which she was to lose either a father or a loved one.

A-Wah-Noh stationed himself beneath a big tree and there remained motionless, awaiting the coming of his opponent. In time he heard stealthy steps approaching. He grasped the axe he carried in a firm grip, tensed for the moment. Nearer and nearer came the footsteps. Soon he could distinguish in the night the outline of a human form. One strong stroke, a heavy fall, and it was done. With savage exultation A-Wah-Noh hewed off the head of his victim and carried it to a clear space at the edge of the lake. There he looked down at the bloody head. Horror of horrors, it was the face of his beloved daughter!

With a terrible cry of anguish, A-Wah-Noh hurled the severed head out into the lake, fled the tribe, and was never seen again, dead or alive. O-We-Tah found the headless body of his sweetheart and disappeared forever. The whole tribe of the Ottawa deserted the lake.

Ever since the place has been known as Haunted Lake because every year on the Feast of the Midsummer Moon the lovely head of Mah-Na-Tah rises out of the waters calling for her beloved O-We-Tah.

The Spell of the Enchanted Well

D) URING the nineteenth century when the Irish immigrated to Canada by the thousands, they brought with them their penchant for story-telling, their unique and inimitable sense of humor, their superstitions and folk tales.

"But did they bring their wee folk, their leprechauns, their fairies?" I once asked an Irish immigrant I knew, a Dubliner born and raised before she came to the Ottawa Valley.

"Bah, no!" she exclaimed. "We left all that nonsense behind us in the Old Sod."

But fairy activities have been documented by various Irish settlers from the 1850s onwards when a man named J.B. McNamee, interviewed in the *Ottawa Citizen*, reported a first sighting.

McNamee lived on the Perth to Westport Road about seven miles west of Perth. The McNamee farm was at the foot of the mountain, just beyond the Scotch Line, not far from Stanleyville. His story of fairy sightings came from his father, a charcoal burner, working the west side of the mountain, close to Westport, with a man named George Murphy. Charcoal burning was an ancient process whereby the wood laid out in layers in a pit would be set well alight, but then covered by a bed of sand or earth so that the wood would be merely charred instead of being burned. This charcoal was an important source of fuel at the time.

One morning when McNamee's father and George Murphy went to work they found the earth they had put over the charcoal pit covered with tiny human footprints. The prints were about two-inches long and exactly the shape of a human foot. The marks of the heel and the ten toes were clear cut. Both McNamee and Murphy knew they had had a special visitation from the fairies.

Another Irishman named Con McCarthy documented a fairy sighting in Gloucester Township south of Ottawa near the Metcalfe Road. When McCarthy was about thirteen, he was walking along the Bowesville Road one night with his friend Frank McBride and several other young fellows. Suddenly their attention was drawn to several miniature red-coated figures which appeared to be floating in the air in a field about forty yards back from the road.

"We stood spellbound and watched their antics," said Mr. McCarthy. "At times they would come down to the ground, clasp their hands and dance around in a circle, not uttering a word; then they would rise into the air several feet and bob up and down. Finally, after about twenty minutes of this procedure, they disappeared as though into the heavens. Now I want to say that we lads hadn't been having a dream — we all saw it together — nor had we been sampling the family cup of good cheer. When I told my father about it later, he said, 'Well, son, you have seen the fairies.'"

In 1936, again in the *Ottawa Citizen*, Mrs. Melinda Graham (nee Bigelow) reported having seen and heard the fairies some seventy years before she was interviewed. A native of Glen Almond on the Lièvre River, ten miles north of Buckingham, Quebec, Mrs. Graham's memory went back to the time when Glen Almond was an isolated community hemmed in by such impenetrable forest that the only means the settlers had of reaching Buckingham for supplies or help was by a blazed trail through the forest, or by canoes hewn out of logs.

Mrs. Graham documented that the fairies existed at Glen Almond.

"I know they did," she said, "because I often heard them talking in the bush back of old Dick Newton's place on the Lièvre, a little above the village. You could never see them, but you could hear them talking to each other in a strange language.

"Old Dick Newton used to tell that the fairies often put his oats in the barn for him at night, providing he left a good meal out for them on the kitchen table before retiring. In the morning the oats were in the barn and the heaped up dishes on the kitchen table were as clean as a whistle.

"Bill Newton's daughter insisted that she heard the fairies at the dishes, but she never ventured to spy on them for fear she would drive them away. She always backed up her father's statement that some mysterious agency was responsible for bringing in the oats and both thoroughly believed in the working fairies."

But the very most amazing and scary story about fairies is the Legend of the Enchanted Well.

NOW, one of the oldest settled communities in Ontario is below The Thousand Islands in the county of Leeds, an area settled largely by the Scots. There, today, the ruins of an historic stone tower stand as a landmark. In the early days this stone tower was used as a grist mill, and a little settlement grew up around it. On a hill not far from the stone tower on the north side of the River Road, the precious hamlet provided clear sparkling water for both inhabitants and wayfarers. Weary, thirsty stagecoach travelers en route between Montreal and Toronto stopped to drink at this well. Gypsy caravans paused to load up their stone jugs. Mother Barnes, the Witch of Plum Hollow, not only quenched her thirst here but also was said to have communed with the fairies at the site which, gradually over the years, became known as the Enchanted Well.

Now, during the era of the French rule in Canada, messengers were on their way with gold to pay the soldiers engaged in battle with the British near Fort Niagara when they were surrounded by hostile Natives. For safekeeping, the French soldiers hurriedly buried the gold in the root system of a huge tree, in the vicinity of the Enchanted Well, intending to return for it later. They were overwhelmed in the confrontation with the Natives, though, and never returned to claim the treasure.

Some time after this event, a Leeds farmer named MacMillan was drinking at the Enchanted Well when the fairies appeared before him and told him he would find a treasure of gold at the roots of a huge tree when he was clearing and stumping his land.

Well, it so happened that one day MacMillan was having great difficulty excavating the stump of a huge tree in a field he was clearing. He was about to heap brush on it and burn it out when he suddenly remembered what the fairies had told him at the Enchanted Well up the road. He dug deep around the roots of the stubborn tree, struck an iron vessel, opened it, and, to his amazement, discovered an enormous cache of French gold coins.

For many years, Farmer MacMillan kept the secret of his gold treasure to himself. In fact, he guarded the secret of his discovery, fearing that someone might appear to claim the gold, or that some government agent would appear to confiscate it. He quietly bought up the surrounding farms, taking the gold coinage necessary for the purchases out of his buried treasure. In the midst of a huge tract of land he eventually built one of the most magnificent residences in Glengarry county, still standing to this day.

Farmer MacMillan died without ever revealing to anyone the hidden source of his unending flow of cash. After his death, descendants found in the rafters of the attic an old manuscript telling the story of his find and enclosing a map showing the site of the iron vessel with the French gold coins. But, alas, the rain and dampness had blotted out the details and the mice had eaten through the paper.

Glengarry Scotsmen have been digging for the past hundred years around the Enchanted Well but, so far, without any luck. The iron vessel with its remaining gold coins has eluded even treasure hunters with Geiger counters.

The Frozen Ghosts of Point Fortune

MANY many years ago when the only highways in Canada were the rivers, Colonel John MacDonnell retired from the North-West Company as a wealthy fur-trader and built himself a mansion on the Ottawa River at Point Fortune near Montreal.

There he lavishly entertained all his neighbors from both the Ontario and Quebec sides of the river, as well as all the dignitaries, travelers from Europe, even English noblemen and royalty who used the river as a highway.

Naturally, since Squire MacDonnell was a Scot, the grandest feast of all was November 30th, St. Andrew's Day. Indeed, it was a double celebration because it was also the Colonel's birthday.

Every year at the Colonel's invitation, a crowd of French-Canadians from the Quebec side of the Ottawa River came over to join in the singing, dancing and drinking necessary to honor the patron saint of Scotland.

One year, unwilling to end their festivities, in the wee small hours of the morning the Scots decided to see their French-Canadian friends home by rowing them over the Ottawa in a big flat-bottomed barge. So all the French-Canadians, many of their young Scottish hosts and hostesses, the pipers and the whisky were all loaded on board. The merry Scots sang out "Auld Lang Syne" to their French-Canadian friends on the Quebec side, and then started back towards home.

Now, as sometimes happens at that time of year in the Ottawa Valley, the temperature dropped drastically in a few hours. However, the Scottish revelers on board the scow, still warmed as they no doubt were by the finest of Scotch whiskies, remained oblivious of the encroaching freeze-up. But when the scow got stuck fast in the ice the celebrants instantly realized their fate.

The grave Scots set all the remaining whisky in the middle of the barge, called on the pipers to play their merriest tunes, and resumed dancing and singing as through tomorrow were another day. It is said that the sound of their revelry echoed to listeners standing on both shores of the Ottawa River. And they sang until the last word was frozen on their lips. And they danced until the last dancer was frozen in place and the last finger of the piper was frozen on his bagpipe.

And it is said to this day that about freeze-up time on the Ottawa River near Point Fortune you can still hear the echoes of those brave singers, dancers, and pipers as they celebrate St. Andrew's Day.

But towards dawn all becomes silent as ice.

The Witch-Canoe of the Ottawa River

OH, there are many strange stories about the Devil on earth in the early days in Canada, many strange and very scary stories that are told and retold, stories about the Devil and the Witch-Canoe, the Devil and the Magic Fiddler, the Devil who abducted Rose Latulippe from her home, the Devil who honeymooned on the Ottawa River, the Devil locked up at Chalk River who even today is waiting to get out. In the early days in Canada, in both French and English, far more people believed in the power of the Devil and many people saw him, usually in disguise, felt his evil influence, or even fell under his spell.

IT IS NOT known how many shantymen left their lonely lumber camps on New Year's Eve in the famous witch-canoe which traveled through the air and was driven by the Devil. But this is how it usually happened.

New Year's Eve, a time to be with loved ones. The lonely woodsmen would be lying on their bunks in the depths of the pine forest, far from anywhere, longing for home, or a sweetheart, or a wife. Suddenly a voice from a foreman or a camp leader (the voice of the Devil in disguise) would say, "Wouldn't you like to see your girl tonight?" "Wouldn't you like to celebrate at your village dance?" "Wouldn't you like to see your wife and children?"

Well, who might not be tempted to sell his soul to the Devil for a chance like that?

"How?" the shantymen would cry out. "We are hundreds of miles from home. It would take us days to walk out, or even go by horse and sleigh."

"Never mind," the tempter would say. "We will take the witch-canoe and journey home. We'll be back in camp by six in the morning."

Then some of the men, tempted by the Devil in disguise and his blandishments, in the magic numbers of two, four, six, or eight, would head for the canoe, ready their paddles, and prepare to levitate into the cold and starry sky of the New Year. But first there was always an oath they had to take:

"Satan, ruler of Hell, we promise to surrender our souls to you if, within the next six hours, we pronounce the name of God your Lord and ours, or if we touch a cross on a church steeple on our journey. On this condition, Satan, ruler of hell, you will transport us back again to camp in the witch-canoe."

The oath being made with the Devil, the witch-canoe rose above the lumber camp, over the white pine forests, over the mountain and rivers, sailing to home, wherever that might be.

If they did not take the name of the Lord in vain or if they did not touch a cross en route, they visited their loved ones and returned at dawn through fading stars and lightening skies in the witch-canoe to their lumber camps, aided and abetted by the Devil.

THE DEVIL seemed to have been an omnipresence in the legends of French-Canadians. One of the most famous of these legends is about Rose Latulippe, the beautiful young girl who flirted with the Devil at Mardi Gras, although she was already engaged to a young man named Gabriel from her village.

Now, Mardi Gras in French-Canadian legends was a celebration of gargantuan feasting and dancing, both Devil temptations, followed immediately by forty days of austere fasting and penitence during Lent.

It so happened many years ago in a village near Montreal, Farmer Latulippe had invited his whole neighborhood to celebrate Mardi Gras with him and his adored daughter, Rose, then age sixteen. Farmer Latulippe let it be known to all his guests that exactly on the stroke of midnight all festivities must cease, for the next day was Ash Wednesday, a holy day, followed by Lent.

That night the fiddler was tireless, almost obsessed it seemed, and the dancing never stopped until eleven o'clock when there came a great knocking at the door. When Farmer Latulippe opened it, there stood a dark, elegantly dressed stranger saying that he had lost his way in the storm and was seeking shelter. Behind him a magnificent black horse tossed his mane.

Of course, Farmer Latulippe invited the lost wayfarer into his home. Both food and drink were refused by the visitor. He simply asked that Rose dance with him. That she did. And they danced like whirling dervishes together, Rose refusing all other offers from partners, even her fiancé Gabriel. At the stroke of twelve, as instructed, all other dancers immediately left the dance floor. But not Rose and her dark partner. In front of the eyes of the shocked gathering, they danced on and on, right into Ash Wednesday. The fiddler, usually a faith-abiding man, played on as though gripped by some internal spell.

Rose and the dark seducer danced until she lost consciousness in his arms. Her garments melted away from her body. The dark handsome young man was transformed into the Devil. Bearing Rose naked in his arms he passed through the door of Farmer Latulippe and disappeared again into the stormy night whence he had come.

INDEED, the Devil did so well throughout Ontario and Quebec that, when he decided to get married, he went up the beautiful Ottawa River with his new bride on their honeymoon. He stopped at one of the pristine sandy beaches which stretch along the hundreds of miles of that mighty river and helped his bride climb a very high hill which came to a plateau on its top, making a magnificent lookout across the Ottawa Valley.

As a very special treat, the Devil had prepared his favorite onion sandwiches. After the picnic some of the onion sandwiches were left behind; these onions sprouted into what is called the Devil's Garden. Explorers, voyageurs, surveyors, canoeists, and boaters traveling along the Ottawa for the past four hundred years have been searching for the Devil's Garden. But, so far, no one has found it. Indeed, it is said by some searchers that the Devil's Garden is so enchanted it moves every year to a new place along the River.

The Devil and his bride continued on their honeymoon up the Ottawa River. But just south of Haileybury the Devil decided he had had enough of marriage. He had given it a try. It was not at all what he had expected and he had grown tired of his new bride. Ruthlessly, he turned her into stone. And there she is to this very day, a high dangerous bluff known to all boaters along the Ottawa as the Devil's Rock.

IT IS well known that often the Devil punished wrong-doers for the rest of time. There is a really scary story about a great blasphemer named Telesphore Tousant who came from St. Cecile-de-Masham and who worked for years and years in a Gillies' lumber camp on the Jocko River which runs into the Ottawa. And he really was a great blasphemer. He constantly broke the Fifth commandment by taking the Lord's name in vain. He said things like "Bitch of Satan," and "God damn you to hell," and "You devilish hag of a daughter of Judas Iscariot," and "the Devil take you."

Now many of the shantymen who worked with Tousant didn't like his great blasphemies and swearings. This was so much against their religion they didn't even want to be within hearing of Tousant. They also thought that the presence of such a sinner amongst them would bring bad luck to their camp, even invite the Devil. They used to say over and over again to Tousant, "The Lord will strike you down, Telesphore, if you don't stop swearing like that."

But Tousant couldn't stop swearing. He continued his terrible blasphemous language so much so that one day the Lord did, indeed, strike him down while he was working with his pike-pole on a log jam, and Telesphore drowned in the Jocko River. Of course, like all great sinners, he went straight to the Devil. The Devil told him his punishment.

"Telesphore Tousant," the Devil said, "You will haunt the Jocko River for the rest of time."

For some years after his drowning, the ghost of Telesphore frequented his old Gillies' lumber camp on the Jocko River. The shantymen said that at night his ghost often came right into the sleep camp, always entering through the roof above their heads. They said he had lost his voice as punishment for so much swearing and blaspheming during his lifetime, but he kept trying to communicate with them through a kind of ghostly sign language made with bony fingers. His old comrades said, "Telesphore is probably trying to say he is sorry. But it is too late."

After the trees had all been cut down, the lumber camps had all fallen into ruins, and the brave shantymen and rivermen had all passed into history, Telesphore had nowhere to haunt but the shores of the Jocko River. And there he wanders still, looking for somebody to talk to him. When you are canoeing the Jocko River and you see a wandering ghost making sign language to you with his bony fingers, you will know you have met up with Telesphore Tousant, the great blasphemer, condemned by the Devil to eternal punishment.

BEFORE the Natives got Christianity, they knew nothing of the Devil. But the Black Robes convinced many Indians to change their religion to Roman Catholicism, in which the Devil plays such a large part.

Now many years ago the land around Chalk River, which runs into the Ottawa, was a favorite hunting ground for the Algonquin tribes. The whole area teemed with game: deer and moose for food; beaver and rabbit for skins for teepees, blankets, clothing; porcupines for quills for all kinds of household uses and decorations.

Then suddenly this great hunting ground became haunted.

"Do not go there any more," one Indian would warn another. "The Chalk River area is haunted. Evil things will happen to you."

"Haunted by what?" the other Indians would ask.

"I have seen it," one Indian would tell another. "It is haunted by a Devil in the shape of a huge ball of fire with an open hand in the center."

Other Indians began to see this haunting image. Gradually, all the hunting grounds of the Chalk River area became deserted. The Natives would not even travel the river any more.

Then the White Man came and settled the Chalk River district. He captured the Devil in the shape of a huge ball of fire with an open hand in the center. The White Man put the Devil in an enormous concrete cage with many many hands controlling the huge ball of fire.

And there the Devil remains to this day, waiting to get out.

The Specter of the Widow Holly

SINCE the invention of the camera, many people have been frightened by having their picture taken. In almost every culture in the world, legends and superstitions about photographs abound. In many primitive societies people are afraid to have their photographs taken because they believe that part of their soul will be lost in the process, in much the same manner that people even today say "Bless you!" when you sneeze so that part of your precious soul does not escape.

I remember years ago in Ireland when attempting to photograph a gypsy caravan, I was chased away with verbal threats and brandished sticks. I have been shown photographs of large pioneer families (usually in two rows, back row standing, front row sitting), with an empty space between two members of the family (usually back row, standing). When I asked why this space was empty, it was explained to me that the person was missing from the portrait because the individual was about to die and presumably had already passed out of the magic reach of the camera. On other occasions, I have been shown a milky ghostly presence behind or between the other faces in large family portraits, again indicating an imminent death. There may be another explanation for these mysteries — in almost every culture it is believed that ghosts and witches cannot be photographed.

In my travels I have been told two remarkable scary tales having to do with images. One was told to me in the Eganville library after a session of telling ghost stories. When I was finished, I asked the audience if they had any scary tales to exchange with me. A young woman from the area rose to tell this story about one of her ancestors.

ABOUT the turn of the century in the Ottawa Valley a large group of immigrants came out from Germany to join the already-established settlement called Germanicus on the Opeongo Line, among them a young woman named Irma Haas. She had had to leave members of her clan behind her in her native land when she decided to come to Canada, but she brought many of her family portraits with her. These were not little snapshots of a photograph album but huge enlarged portraits set in wide heavy gilt and embossed frames.

Shortly after her arrival Irma Haas married a young man named Tobias Holly whose family also had settled the Opeongo Line. When they took up house, Irma hung her huge heavy family portraits throughout the Holly residence. For many years the Haas ancestors looked down on Irma and Tobias Holly's life as they worked their farm, raised their many children, and grew old together. When Tobias died first, as men usually do, and Irma was left a widow alone, she went to live with her youngest daughter Gretchen and her husband Harry Berrigan on the Opeongo Line. And, of course, she took all her huge heavy gilt-framed family portraits with her and hung them up once again, this time in the Berrigan household.

A quarter of a century went by and Widow Holly passed her ninetieth birthday. When she felt in her bones that she was nearing the end of her life, she made her daughter promise her that, when she died, the family portraits would be placed in the bottom of her casket and buried with her. It was her greatest fear that they would be destroyed or thrown out, for she felt that they had no great meaning to anyone except herself, particularly when she saw how little regard some of her grandchildren and great-grandchildren had for their roots and their heritage.

Shortly after Gretchen made the promise, Widow Holly died. But the family did not know what to do about putting all those heavy gilt-framed portraits into the casket with her. Somehow it just didn't seem right — at least, to some members of the family. Everyone had grown quite used to them around the house. And what was the point in preserving them for so many years only to have them all rot in the grave? Besides, now they were worth money, especially to the antique dealers.

Quickly the Haases, the Hollys, and the Berrigans held a family meeting. But they could not agree on what to do with the portraits. Finally someone had a brilliant idea. They should go to the parish priest and ask his advice. After all, he knew what should go into a Christian grave and all about promises unkept.

When Father Tom Hunt was approached about the matter and told the whole story, he threw up his hands and exclaimed, "What utter nonsense! Whoever heard of such foolishness. Go home and forget all about it!"

So Widow Holly was buried at Cormac — without her family portraits. After the funeral all the relatives and friends trooped to the Berrigan house to mourn their loss and feast upon all the good food provided by the neighbors for the wake.

And while they were all gathered together at the death-house, there was suddenly heard this terrible thudding and crashing throughout the whole place as all of Widow Holly's family portraits fell to the floor and smashed into a thousand pieces.

THE SECOND scary story about photographs was told to me by a woman in Glengarry, a mature student who was working at the University of Ottawa on her Ph.D thesis. For this thesis, she had to travel in Montreal and Quebec City to do research, interviewing old people in Ontario and Quebec about their attitudes towards the church and its teachings. After she interviewed the old-timers she photographed each of them for her records.

So, one time she interviewed this little old lady from Vankleek Hill, itself a very scary place because, as everyone knew, there was a man living there who was building a rocket to go to the moon in his basement. When the woman from the university had finished her interview she sat the little old lady down in her little old rocking chair in her living room surrounded by all her little old mementoes and memorabilia, trinkets and bric-a-brac, and she took her photograph with the same camera and the same film she had used in all her other interviews.

Then the university woman had the photos developed in the usual place and got back her prints. All the other photographs in the roll were as expected. But not the one of the little old lady from Vankleek Hill. Everything was in its place in the living room as it had been on the day she took the photograph, all the furniture, all the mementoes and memorabilia, all the pictures on the wall. But there was no little old lady in the rocking chair.

"Oh, dear," said the woman from the university. "My flash must have been faulty. That means I will have to go back and do the photo again."

So the woman from the university went back to the little old lady in Vankleek Hill to photograph her again in her rocking chair. She took the photo, only this time without using her flash.

But when she had the print developed, there was the little old rocking chair sitting on the verandah of the little old lady's house in Vankleek Hill. But there was no little old lady sitting in her rocking chair!

Yes, you have to remember that witches can never be photographed.

The Thronging Ghosts of Ghost Hill

of Ghost Hill

& OTHER SPOOKY STORIES

The Thronging Ghosts of Ghost Hill

ALONG Highway 148 outside of Aylmer, Quebec, and just south of Breckenbridge Bridge, St. Augustine's Church, a little stone building built in 1874, virtually sits on the road. Just past this site is the infamous Ghost Hill, a long sweeping grade with mysteriously tangled bush on both sides and, at the top of the hill before you go down into the "banshees," an easy-to-miss hidden lane leads up to the House on Ghost Hill, an old stone dwelling almost hidden from view at the foot of the Gatineaus. This hill is so haunted and has been haunted for so long that even today there are people who will not travel it, or, if they do have to travel it, will certainly never do it alone or at night.

Since the 1800s, along this stretch of Highway 148 weird things have happened, both in broad daylight and in the dead of night. White-faced farmers raced home to tell their wives of wagon wheels that refused to budge on Ghost Hill. Horses there took sudden frights, upsetting carts and drivers, sometimes injuring them. Eerie and uncanny noises were heard in the trees on both sides of Ghost Hill. Not infrequently, a strange light would be seen by teamsters a few yards in front of their horses, only to disappear as the drivers approached it. Sometimes the eerie light would move from in front of horses to behind the rig or wagon. One man saw the devil jump into his car, horns, tail, spear, and all.

Over the past two centuries many people have reported hearing wailing sounds or seeing white filmy figures floating along the edges of the road at Ghost Hill. Even today many people are afraid to travel up or down Ghost Hill because so many bizarre accidents, even murders, have occurred along it, and so many ghosts still stalk it.

Early in the 1800s, on a dark gloomy gray day in the fall, a young man who lived near Ghost Hill went walking in Isaac Lusk's woods with his gun, hoping to catch a partridge or two. In the distance, right on Ghost Hill, he saw a cow approaching him. As it started to charge at him in a peculiar way, he realized there was something wrong with it and shot it.

When he got up to the cow, to his horror he discovered that he had shot his best friend who had put on a cow's hide to play a practical joke.

The body of the practical joker disappeared and his soul went into an old gnarled tree that stood on the site of the tragedy. The tree became haunted with the soul of the dead young man. Afterwards so many accidents were attributed to the ghost in the old gnarled tree on Ghost Hill that, finally, in 1830, pioneer Lusk had to cut it down.

A few years later two men from Luskville were returning late to their homes after drinking heavily in an Aylmer hotel. Driving homewards in the dark with horses and hay-wagon a heated argument arose between the two men. One man killed the other with a pitchfork right on Ghost Hill. And the ghost of the murdered drunk joined the other ghosts on Ghost Hill.

In the year 1885, Jim Boyer who lived at Black Bay on the Ottawa River near Luskville, went to the Aylmer market to sell his farm produce. He did well that day with his butter, pork, and vegetables and was returning home along Highway 148, alone in the dark, with his money jingling in his pockets, thinking of what he might buy with all his profits. But right on Ghost Hill he was robbed and murdered. The robbers were caught, taken to jail, and eventually tried for their crimes. But the judge declared the robbery and the murder "unpremeditated" and the men were freed. Jim Boyer's ghost then joined the throng on Ghost Hill, but it was always said you could tell him from all the others because he was calling out for justice.

Once upon a misty autumn night, oh, perhaps fifty years ago, an Eardley farmer named Wyman McKechnie was walking home late at night. There was a harvest moon above him, but the wind was blowing occasional clouds across the skies. As the moonlight came and went upon his path in a heavily wooded area near Ghost Hill, he thought for a moment he could see an eerie-looking object behind him, a fuzzy floating form sheathed in a white cloak.

Frightened somewhat, McKechnie quickened his pace but, when he did this, the specter immediately sped up to the same pace. McKechnie broke into a run; but so did the apparition. Faster and faster McKechnie ran with the ghost close on his heels.

Finally, out of breath, McKechnie was forced to halt and sit down on one end of a big hollow log. Immediately, the ghost sat down on the other end.

"Well," said the ghost to McKechnie, "we were certainly going some there."

"Yes!" cried the terrified McKechnie, leaping to his feet. "And now that I've got my breath we'll go some more!"

McKechnie finally beat the ghost home. But even to this day travelers on Ghost Hill sometimes have to outrun the marathon ghost who likes to race.

The Witches and Witch Doctors of Eardley

NOW back in the pioneer days in Canada you could not go to the corner store to buy a pound of butter. There was no corner store and you had to make your own butter from your own cows' cream. It was hard work; you made it in a large wooden churn with a dasher which you pounded up and down until the cream turned into delicious butter, homemade butter, better than anything you can buy in the corner stores today.

This is a story about Farmer Flear of Eardley who suddenly, for no reason he could fathom, began to fail to get any butter from his churning. He had his whole family take turns at the old dasher, in case there was a hex on one of the members. But try as they all might, none of them could make the farmer's butter "come," in much the same manner that sometimes whipping cream does not whip no matter how hard you beat it.

"Why don't you send for one of the Witches of Eardley? Your cows are obviously bewitched," said neighbor Bradley.

Farmer Flear, who considered himself an educated man, laughed at such a foolish suggestion.

"Who would ever believe in all that craziness about witches," he answered neighbor Bradley, and then went home and told his wife about Bradley's silly idea. But his wife didn't poo-poo the suggestion at all as he had expected. Instead, she raised an eyebrow and said, "Maybe he has something. It worked for the Hodgins, didn't it?"

"I didn't think you were as crazy as the rest of them," Farmer Flear flung at his wife, and went out to the barn to look at his poor cows again.

But, finally in desperation, when his family had been out of butter for weeks and complaining bitterly, he sent for one of the Witches of Eardley who lived alone — witches always live alone — far up the Back Mountain Road. After the visitation from the Witch, Farmer Flear's butter from his wife's churnings began again to "come regular," and the farmer's wife had butter to spread on her homemade bread, butter for her homemade cookies and cakes, butter for her hot oatmeal porridge in the mornings.

Now, no harm would have come of this whole unhexing except that the Witch, in order to prove her powers, told Farmer Flear that the man who had bewitched his cows would come within eight days to visit him and to borrow something. Well, one day, would you believe, one of the farmer's most trusted neighbors ran out of beans for bean soup and came over to borrow a mess of them well within the eight days of the Witch's prediction. Right then and there Farmer Flear broke off the friendship of a lifetime with his neighbor.

And it is always said that the borrowing of beans in Eardley has been quite unknown from that time to this.

ALONG with the Bradleys, the Lusks, the Sallys, the Nugents, the Armstrongs, and the Merrifields, the Hayworths were very early settlers in Eardley, settling along the Ottawa River about 1850. The original old Hayworth farm was on the riverside of Highway 148 near Ghost Hill, a landmark on the road between Aylmer and Quyon. It is still there today and still lived in by Hayworth descendants who can tell you all the stories about the Witches and Witch Doctors of Eardley.

Now, one time years ago all the cattle on the Hayworth farm stopped producing any milk, a disaster in those pioneer days because you had to have milk for babies, for children, for sick baby lambs, for mixing in pig feed, for baking and cooking. The Hayworths suspected their cattle had been hexed by a very old and very cross widow living in their area. They were going to call in the local Witches of Eardley but then they heard about this Witch Doctor far over the mountains at Wakefield on the Gatineau River who was supposed to be more powerful than any of the local talent. So they sent for him.

The Witch Doctor from Wakefield arrived at the Hayworth farm and immediately sent for flanges to bleed a pure white horse. Then he sent out for the hairs from the mane of a black horse, certainly easier to find than a pure white horse. He boiled the blood and the hairs together until they became an evil-smelling gooey concoction.

He then ordered Farmer Hayworth to bore holes in all his cedar rail fence posts which bordered on the road. Together the Witch Doctor and Farmer Hayworth plugged the boiled hair and blood concoction into all the bored holes to remove the hex placed upon the cattle in the fields. Within a few days, Farmer Hayworth's cows were all milking again and the Witch Doctor returned to Wakefield, his reputation greatly enhanced and now spread over the mountains into a new territory.

That was all a long time ago. But if you go along that cedar fence today bordering the road near Ghost Hill, you can still see all the bored holes made there by the Wakefield Witch Doctor in order to unhex the Hayworth cows. Inside the holes, if you look carefully, you can still see — and smell — the gooey concoction made from the blood of a pure white horse and the hairs from the mane of a black horse.

WELL, shortly afterwards it happened again in Eardley that another farmer by the name of Merrifield failed also to get any butter from the cream of his cows. But Farmer Merrifield was not a man to hesitate and be indecisive. He immediately sent for one of the Witches of Eardley. Unfortunately, it so happened that all the Witches of Eardley who lived close at hand were busy. He got instead the Witch Doctor from Wakefield across the mountains. This Witch Doctor had long wanted to return to Eardley to do another unhexing there. He arrived in record time — it would almost seem that he flew over the mountains — and looked very wise, certainly wise enough to make you want to put your trust in him for unhexing your cows.

But, believe it or not, after a series of incantations and attempts, he finally said to Farmer Merrifield, "This spell cast on your cows is far too magical and far too strong for me. I must go to a far away country to collect new powers."

"Where is that country?" the farmer asked the Witch Doctor.

"It is so far away," replied the Witch Doctor, "that I cannot make the journey for I haven't any money."

"How much will it take?" asked the butterless farmer, secretly very worried that one so powerful had cast a spell over his whole herd of cattle.

"It will take nearly thirty dollars," said the Witch Doctor.

"But I don't have thirty dollars to my name!" exclaimed Farmer Merrifield. "What on earth must I do?"

"You must borrow it," calmly replied the Witch Doctor.

Now all this happened in Eardley long before the borrowing of either beans or money had gone out of style. So the poor farmer went off to a rich neighbor named Nugent, borrowed the thirty dollars, and sent the Witch Doctor off to regain his powers in a far country.

Before the Witch Doctor left, the farmer said to him, "If I give you the thirty dollars to go to a foreign country to get new powers, how do I know you will return to unhex my poor cows?"

"I give you my word," said the Witch Doctor.

So the farmer put his faith in the word of the Witch Doctor, for, in those early days, every man's word was as binding as the bond between mother and child.

Within a few weeks, true to his word, the Witch Doctor returned from the foreign country, bringing with him a new batch of powers that would easily beat up on the Devil himself.

"Now to work," said the Witch Doctor, rolling up his sleeves. "First, put the churn in the middle of the floor. Next, tie a log-chain around the churn. To the other end of the log-chain fasten the iron colter of a plough. Build a roaring fire in your wood stove. Put the colter on the stove. Sit down and wait. The neighbor who has been doing all these evil things to your cattle will come running over to your farm like one possessed and try to get into your house. Don't let him in or my spell will be broken."

All the Witch Doctor's directions were carefully followed. Farmer Merrifield was sitting by his wood stove patiently waiting when a neighbor man came running up to the house. The neighbor pounded all the doors and tried all the windows just like someone possessed. But Farmer Merrifield's doors and windows held fast and the possessed neighbor was never seen again.

The Witch Doctor liked Eardley so much that he stayed. He was so grateful to Farmer Merrifield who borrowed the thirty dollars to send him to a foreign country to regain his powers that he took on the farmer's debt and repaid it himself. The Witch Doctor never returned to Wakefield, and ever after made his living in Eardley. And still does, to this very day.

Indeed, the Witches and Witch Doctors have never left Eardley. Sometimes, on a magical night when the moon is full and the sky is very still you will hear a rustling along Highway 148 going from Aylmer to Quyon, and particularly near Ghost Hill. If you look up and it's your lucky night, you will see the Witches of Eardley over the mountains. Witches, of course, can fly.

The Witch Doctors are still there too, but, of course, they cannot fly. They have gone deep into the forest, into little lonely mountain huts where they keep their unhexing concoctions, their herbs and charms, the secrets of their powers all ready for the next time they are needed in Eardley.

The Assyrian Peddler of Luskville

FOR many, many years in the early days of Canada, the Assyrian peddler, with his huge pack on his back, was a familiar sight walking the roads and country lanes. There was great excitement when he came to your house or your farm. He would throw down his huge pack and open it so that all could behold its wonders — new pots, darning needles, alarm clocks, ribbons for your hair, trinkets, treasures, even toys.

Now, one time long ago this Assyrian peddler was walking one of the most beautiful roads in the Ottawa Valley, the road that winds between the Ottawa River and the Gatineau Hills from Aylmer, Quebec, to Chapeau.

That day he had walked from Aylmer to nearby Luskville. It had been a very good day and he had collected a great deal of money in gold coins. He intended to stay the night at a stopping-place run by two weird old wicked sisters who were said to be some of the Witches of Eardley. They could cast spells, put hexes on butter, and mix strange brews for all kinds of Devil's diseases.

Now, in those early days, of course, there were no policemen, and people were often robbed as they slept in the stopping-places. Because of this, the Assyrian peddler always buried his money somewhere near by, slept his night at the stopping-place, dug his money up in the morning, and then went on his way. That night he buried all his gold coins at the foot of three big scraggly pines on Ghost Hill.

During the night the two old weird wicked sisters murdered the Assyrian peddler and threw his body in the well. But before they did that, they must have wrung out of him a confession that he did not have his money on him, but had buried it at the foot of three big scraggly pines.

For years afterwards the two sisters were seen digging around the foot of any three big scraggly pine trees they could find anywhere. And there were a lot of them back in those early days. But the two weird old wicked sisters died without ever finding the treasure.

Then, many years later, around 1900, a man from Luskville named Howdy Moore went to the Aylmer Fair and there he had his fortune told by a gypsy fortune-teller.

"You will find the gold of the Assyrian peddler at the base of three big scraggly pine trees on a hill," she told him.

By this time there were not many groups of three big scraggly pines left in the whole country. So Howdy Moore went to the base of three big scraggly pines on Ghost Hill and dug. And there he found great handfuls of gold coins buried there by the Assyrian peddler so many many years ago when he walked with his pack of wonders from Aylmer to Luskville.

The Man with the Rabbit's Eye

BACK in the early days in the Ottawa Valley when every farm was a working farm, traveling or Assyrian peddlers could make a good living going door-to-door selling all kinds of household knick-knacks. As these peddlers moved from district to district, they heard all sorts of stories and picked up all the local gossip. Some of these peddlers became renowned as great storytellers, particularly if they were Irish and expert at drawing "the long bow."

The pioneer farmers were often isolated from their neighbors or working too hard to do much visiting around, so they especially welcomed the storytelling peddlers and often kept them overnight. Then the whole family would gather in the evenings to listen to the stories the traveling salesman carried with him in his storytelling bag — tall tales, ghostly yarns, recountings of unsolved murders and strange drownings, and the latest gossip collected from the places he had visited.

Paddy Mullarkey was one of the most welcome peddlers in the Townships of Osgoode, Gloucester, and North Gower south of Ottawa, so great a storyteller was he. There was always a good supper and a warm bed for Paddy at the farmhouses in exchange for fireside storytelling that would lighten the long winter nights after he had left.

Now, Big Tom Jinkinson, an Osgoode farmer, decided to play a trick on Paddy when next he came to the Jinkinson area. Big Tom felt some of the tall tales Paddy told were too tall altogether and that some of the gossip was too malicious altogether. Besides, Big Tom considered himself a man of reason and agricultural science and he didn't believe in such nonsense as banshees, third sight, and Irish superstitions. He wanted to prove to Paddy Mullarkey that he, for one, couldn't be taken in and that he wasn't "born yesterday."

So farmer Jinkinson laid his plans to pull the wool over Paddy's eyes, beat him at his own game and even make him look foolish to boot. Big Tom confided in his wife who fully agreed with the plot and who knew, as well as her husband did, that Paddy could neither read nor write, although he could add sums very well.

When Paddy next came to the Jinkinson farm, he was immediately invited to stay the night and sit down to a hearty meal. After supper when the oil lamp was lit, Big Tom pulled out his *Ottawa Journal* and placed it on the cleared kitchen table. Mrs. Jinkinson stoked the kitchen stove and poured a second cup of tea for everyone. Paddy, ready for storytime, pulled out his clay pipe and tobacco pouch. Big Tom studied the paper. Suddenly he exclaimed aloud, "My goodness! Isn't this awful!"

"Oh, tell us!" cried out his wife. "What is so awful?"

Big Tom read aloud from his paper.

"It says here that Mick McKendrick of Osgoode had a shooting accident and lost an eye. He was taken to the big Civic Hospital in Ottawa where Dr. James Grant, a famous physician and eye specialist, said that he could give Mick a new eye through a recent European discovery called transplantation. Mick was said to be greatly pleased at the news and his whole family filled with joy. Consent was given for the transplant operation and the recovery seemed to be going as expected. But when the bandages were removed from Mick's eyes a terrible discovery was made."

It seemed that Mick had been given a rabbit's eye — either through some kind of error or because the good doctor had run short of human eyes.

"Oh, blessed be the saints of Erin!" Mrs. Jinkinson cried out. "Read on, Tom, read on."

"It can't be true. It can't be true," Paddy said.

"You're talking about truth, Paddy Mullarkey! Here, read it yourself," Big Tom said. Paddy, of course, pulled back from this suggestion.

"Oh, no," he said. "You read on, Tom."

Big Tom read on while Paddy Mullarkey's eyes grew wider and wider.

"The paper says that that wasn't the worst of it. Not at all. Since returning home from the hospital Mick has become a terrible pest in his community, slipping into everyone's garden at night and eating all the lettuce and carrots. And it seems now that whenever Mick sees a hound dog or a man carrying a gun, he takes to the bush, running like a rabbit on all fours and looking for a hole to hide in."

Well, Paddy Mullarkey could hardly wait to get on the road the next morning to spread the sensational story of The Man Who Got the Rabbit's Eye. Far and wide he retold the story at every farmhouse fireside. There was much speculation about the evil effects of European imports and experimental medicine. Storytellers took the tale far beyond the Ottawa Valley to places where it was even translated into other languages.

Farmer Jinkinson and his wife died many laughs and many years later taking to the grave the secret of the trick they had played on Paddy Mullarkey. Paddy Mullarkey died many stories and many years later without ever knowing that Big Tom Jinkinson had told him a taller tale than any he had ever retold or invented himself.

But Paddy Mullarkey's name lived on forever in the Ottawa Valley. Whenever people heard a story like The Man Who Got the Rabbit's Eye, they said to the storyteller, "Ah, go on now. Sure, you're full of malarkey."

The Wendigo at Widow Helferty's House

UP on the Mountain Road back in the days when some of the Indians still lived in the Ottawa Valley and the Irish were still flowing into the Gatineau Hills to take up land, there lived a very old lady named Widow Helferty. Widow Helferty lived in a little log house on a half-cleared farm high in the hills off the Mountain Road back of Aylmer, Quebec.

Now when she was very old, past ninety-five, Widow Helferty took very ill and, in true old-time fashion, neighbors began to call, bringing her chicken soup, homemade bread, and apple pies. But then the strangest thing began to happen to all these callers.

Every time any one of them went into Widow Helferty's house they were followed by a peculiar

Click, click, click

all through the house.

Try as they might they could not locate the source of the

Click, click, click.

They searched in the wood-box and behind the stove and under the bed. But the

Click, click, click

could not be explained.

Then one day Mrs. O'Shaunessy, Widow Helferty's neighbor came to visit the log house. The odd

Click, click, click

followed her into the house and then followed her out again, only stopping when she got back to her own farm gate.

On another occasion Paddy Hogan from Hogan's Hill called on old Widow Helferty with some homemade hot cross buns from his wife. The strange

Click, click, click

stayed with him all the time he visited old Widow Helferty, and then the

Click, click, click

followed him right to his front door where he was met by his wife. Even his wife heard the scary

Click, click, click

which did not stop until he was inside his house and had slammed the door.

The story of the bizarre

Click, click, click

in Widow Helferty's house spread far and near and curious and noise-hunting visitors by the score began to turn up at her house. None of them, however, no matter how long they tried or how hard they searched, could find the source of the haunting

Click, click, click

even though it was here, there, and everywhere in Widow Helferty's house and followed her visitors down the road to their farm gates and to their front doors going

Click, click, click.

Finally, there appeared on the scene two young men who were ghost-layers.
They listened very intently to the

> *Click, click, click.*

"We are ghost-layers," they said. "Leave it to us. We will solve the mystery."
They followed the weird

> *Click, click, click*

all through Widow Helferty's house and then they followed the weird

> *Click, click, click*

out the front door and then they opened the garden gate and followed the

> *Click, click, click*

into the garden and then they followed the weird

> *Click, click, click*

all through the garden and then they heard the weird

> *Click, click, click*

leading them across the fields and they followed the weird

> *Click, click, click*

across the fields and then the weird noise led them into the far bush

> *Click, click, click*

and then the weird noise led them through the swamp lands

> *Click, click, click*

and then the weird noise led them over the rocks, up the mountains,
and into the Poltimore Caves

> *Click, click, click*

where the ghost-layers disappeared and never were seen again.

> When the scary
>
> *Click, click, click*

returned to Widow Helferty's house, Alice Snowshoes the wise old Indian of Aylmer,
was called in to listen to the weird

> *Click, click, click*

"That's a Wendigo," she pronounced. "Don't ever try to see it or find it.
You can't. A Wendigo will never show itself."

> The
>
> *Click, click, click*

at Widow Helferty's house continued until the old lady died.

Then the weird

    Click, click, click

ceased as soon as she was buried in the ground in the Mountain Road Cemetery and was never heard again in all of Western Quebec —

    CLICK, CLICK, CLICK

The Woman in White

NOW let me tell you, first of all, that the Gatineau Hills north of Ottawa are among the spookiest areas in the whole of Canada, filled as they are with deep mountain valleys, twisting torturous rivers, secret caves haunted with echoes, deep forests where few human footprints have ever crossed, sunken pioneer cemeteries, and the half-buried crosses of the rivermen who drowned as they rushed the timbers down to the Ottawa River.

Because the first settlers in these hills were from Ireland, fairies, leprechauns, banshees, and ghosts are everywhere. And then there are all those ghosts of the early pioneers, particularly the most famous of the Gatineau ghosts — the Woman in White — who appeared in 1860 in the Township of Egan, named after the early timber baron, Sir Henry Egan.

Back in those days, early Gatineau pioneer James Maloney and his wife Corabella lived at Mercier Chute (or waterfall) on the Desert River. There James ran the grist mill while his wife ran the house and raised their two daughters, Dorothy and Diane. When Corabella died suddenly, James had to run not only his grist mill business but take care of his young children as well, aged only three and five at their mother's death.

One day in early spring only a year after their mother had died, when James was busy at work, the two girls wandered off the millsite and disappeared into the woods. As soon as the discovery was made a few hours later, James raised a hue and cry throughout his neighborhood. Patrick Moore, foreman of Hall's lumber camp three miles away from the millsite, immediately organized a search team made up of some of the most famous woodsmen then in the Gatineau — Tom Budge, Moses Leary, Robert Carney, William Tarrney, and John Michel of the Ottawa tribe.

Led by Moore for many days and nights in damp cold weather, the search team tracked the lost children. All the way up the Desert River, then five miles up the Eagle

River, following where they could the childrens' footprints and even finding the places where they had curled up together in the hollow crotch of a tree or in a bed of leaves. So good were the trackers they could even tell where the children had stopped to sustain themselves on wintergreen berries and wild rose hips. Across bridges, along sand beaches, through laid-down layers of forest leaves, up and down mountainsides, the search party followed the meandering trail, sometimes losing it and giving up hope, then finding it again and pushing onwards.

"Someone must be watching over them," Moore said to his flagging party. "They are still alive. Let us not give up."

And the search went on, day and night, the searchers' voices echoing up the mountains and through the valleys, "Dorothy, Diane, where are you? Dorothy and Diane, where are you?"

But as the days passed some of the searchers began to doubt they would ever find the children, and they wanted to give up and go home.

"Someone must be watching over them," Moore said again, urging them to go on.

"I believe they are still alive," said John Michel, the Ottawa tracker. "It seems like a miracle but the signs say they are still alive."

Then some of the search party took heart because they knew that John Michel could read the woods better than any of them, perhaps better than anyone alive in all the Gatineau Hills. So most of them kept going, following all the signs of the passage of the children until they came to the edge of the great cedar swamp which lies on the shore of Cedar Lake. There their hearts truly fell.

"No one can stay alive in there for very long," said the searchers. "The great cedar swamp is full of all kinds of animals and snakes — very scary for two little girls — and there is no dry place to bivouac at night."

"I believe they are still alive," said John Michel, the tracker. "I know the swamp well. I will go on alone."

On the fifteenth day, John Michel found Dorothy and Diane in the watery reaches of the great cedar swamp, wandering dazed and frightened, but still alive.

"It was the Woman in White," Dorothy mumbled as John Michel wrapped her and her younger sister in his jacket, put them both on his back, and carried them through miles of wilderness to Hall's camp, where some of the weary searchers had gathered to rest and recover, find food and warmth before making their separate journeys home.

When foreman Moore saw John Michel walk out of the bush with the two little girls on his back, he was so happy he broke down and cried.

"It was the Woman in White who saved us," Dorothy kept repeating.

"How did she do that?" Maloney gently asked his daughter.

"Every night she stood by us in the forest when we lay down to sleep and watched over us," Dorothy answered.

"She looked just like mother," said Diane, "and she was all in white — just like an angel."

And it was then that everyone knew that someone had, indeed, been watching over the lost children, and that the Woman in White was the ghost of the young mother watching over her beloved children in danger, bringing them to safety after fourteen days lost in the Gatineau Hills.

The Bedeviled Cat of Breckenridge

JUST what it was about the Eardley district that made it such a rendezvous for spooks, ghosts, witches, and other wild and weird elements of the olden days nobody seems to know. But countless stories are told of mysterious happenings there, particularly in the 1850s, '60s, and '70s, including all kinds of stories about haunted houses. This Eardley tale, dated 1866, was told by an old settler named Thomas Lusk.

Now seventy years ago there was an old log house near where the Ferris family lived, not far from Breckenridge. For a time the house was lived in by Joe Herrington, an old bachelor. While he lived there he said he was nearly driven insane by spookings.

Joe said that after he retired at night he would hear uncanny sounds downstairs. On one occasion he was awakened by a deafening crash, and when he went downstairs, he found all his dishes in small pieces on the floor. On another occasion he hung his clothes up to dry and warm by his stove and went down in the morning to find the clothes torn to shreds and scattered all over the kitchen floor. Finally, Herrington moved out, unable to stand the spooking any longer.

After he moved out, people passing by the house saw lights flashing on and off, heard the rattling of chains and the banging of pots and pans. Reports of this haunted house spread far and wide and people came from everywhere, mostly in the daytime, to see what was going on in Eardley's most famous haunted house.

Then the strangest thing of all happened there — but only to people who were brave enough to pass by or go near the Eardley haunted house at night. A huge black cat began to appear at the windows. Shots were fired at it, but even though they appeared to hit their mark, the cat would appear at another window, maybe an upstairs one this time. Crack marksmen were drawn to the house, challenged to try to hit the elusive black cat. But they always missed. The cat would turn up at another window. For years the great black cat appeared at the windows of the haunted house, sometimes turning its head defiantly towards the onlookers, sometimes sitting on its haunches and licking itself. But the instant a gun was raised, it would magically disappear.

And you have to remember always that ghosts cannot be captured and witches cannot be killed.

The Raising of the Dead at Waltham

ONE time not so very long ago — about 1920 or so, to be exact — three young men drowned at Waltham, Quebec, while crossing the Ottawa River in a rowboat. Try as they might, the families could not find the bodies for burial. And, of course, the parents of the three young men were beside themselves not only with grief but fear as well for they were all Roman Catholics who believed that proper burial in consecrated ground was essential for anyone's passage to heaven.

For days, then weeks, the men from the community searched for the bodies in the river, commandeering all kinds of boats, using grappling hooks, sending down amateur divers. Their gruesome task was made even more difficult by the very nature of the Ottawa River. As a lumber river it was full of sunken logs and dead-heads in which a drowned body could become trapped or lodged. Full of swift currents and many rapids, the river could quickly carry a body downstream and far away.

In those days you could buy dynamite at the general store, and many men of the community who had worked in the mines of the north were adept at its use. As a further method to force the river to give up the dead, dynamite men set off charges along the shoreline in the hope that the disturbances from the blasts would dislodge the bodies and bring them to the surface.

When the dynamite failed, some of the drowned young men's relatives traveled to Ottawa. There they procured from the Department of National Defence a small cannon not being used at the time — the world was between two wars in the 1920s — and brought it to Waltham on a Canadian National Railway flat-car. But even the shooting off of the cannon was not sufficient to cause strong enough reverberations to dislodge the missing bodies.

Finally, professional divers were hired and brought up from Ottawa and Montreal.

But to no avail. Search as they might, the river hung on to the bodies with the stubbornness of evil in the heart of man.

Months had gone by, months which had only heightened the anxiety of the Roman Catholic parents and hardened their determination. The parents went to their parish priest to plead with him for action. Surely he, a man of God, understood their agony. Besides, Father Harrington already had a reputation for performing the impossible. Perhaps faith would succeed where all practical and innovative ways had failed.

"Father Harrington," they begged, "can you please do something to resurrect the bodies of our sons so that we can give them a decent Christian burial and save their souls?"

And they pestered Father Harrington, making his life so unbearable that finally he said, "Meet me at the Ottawa shore at Waltham tomorrow morning and I will see what I can do."

Well, you can imagine how that word spread throughout the countryside and up and down the river! By automobile, by horse and buggy, by foot, people came from everywhere, from far and near to watch Father Harrington rescue the three bodies from their watery prison.

There on the shore of the Ottawa River at Waltham, Quebec, surrounded by crowds of witnesses, Father Harrington blessed the bread, threw it on the water, and said a holy incantation. And before the eyes of the assembly the three bodies of the drowned young men shot up out of the Ottawa River like porpoises, and floated before the astounded eyes of the multitude.

WELL, I put that story told by the old man away in the back of my mind, discarding it as the kind of a miracle I could not quite believe.

Then several years later, I was working with students in an Ottawa High School and, after the session, went into the Staff Room to have coffee with the teachers. A young teacher in her thirties introduced herself to me as a native of Waltham, Quebec. Naturally, we got talking about folk tales and legends in the Valley. After a while she said to me, "Did you ever hear the story of the Raising of the Bodies at Waltham?"

"I think so," I said cautiously, "but please tell it to me again."

And the young teacher repeated the story of Father Harrington at Waltham which had been told to me some years before by the old man at Sheenboro.

When she had finished I asked her, "Where did you hear that story?"

"From my grandmother," she replied. "She was there when it happened."

The Burial of Bandy Burke

& OTHER DARK LEGENDS

The Dripping Seaman

GEORGE Usborne was an English sea captain who came to Canada about 1800 and made his first fortune in timber stands he held along the St. Lawrence River and in the Saguenay River Valley. But he was chased from there by a ghost. And this is how it happened.

Usborne owned three large ocean-going schooners and was engaged in shipping cargoes of square timber from Quebec City to Liverpool in England. He became very wealthy and built a huge stone mansion on the heights at Quebec City for his bride, Ethel Mary Seaton Ogden, an American lady whom he met while on lumbering business in upper New York State.

For a time Usborne prospered honestly. But then he grew greedy. He began to try to make a killing by loading the square timbers not only in the holds of his ships, but also on the decks. In a heavy storm this was fatal because the huge square timbers, sometimes weighing as much as a ton each, slid to one side of the deck and capsized the vessel.

One year Mary and George Usborne chose May 1st to celebrate the end of the drive on the rivers and the departure of Usborne's ships to Liverpool loaded with the great square timbers of the Saguenay River Valley. The celebration was held in the ballroom of the Usborne mansion attended by all the fair women of Quebec's high society wearing gowns imported from London, and by all the grave men of Quebec's high society sampling rare wines imported from Paris.

While all this feasting and dancing was in progress, suddenly there was a loud knocking at the rarely-used ballroom door on the riverside.

All the music stopped. All the merriment ceased. When Mary and George opened the door, there stood a lone man in seaman's garb, dripping water on the doorstep, and covered with seaweed. While everyone stood rooted to the floor, he raised his arm, pointed a long bony finger at George Usborne, opened his mouth as though to cry out an accusation.

Although his lips moved, no words were heard. And the sailor disappeared. No trace of him at all on the doorstep except a pool of water. Just there and gone!

Some time later, George Usborne discovered that his ships had gone down on the night of May 1st, the very night the dripping seaman had appeared at the ballroom door.

George Usborne went bankrupt and, for several years, tried to start again at Quebec City. But Mary didn't want to live any longer in the stone mansion on the heights. It was haunted by the ghost of the dripping seaman who appeared every May 1st on the doorstep of the riverside entrance to the ballroom. George Usborne then tried to sell the beautiful stone mansion, but no one would buy it because it was haunted. So George and Mary had to abandon it. They moved to Portage-du-Fort in the Ottawa Valley where the timber trade was just burgeoning, and there they began anew.

The Wail of Peter White

UP the Ottawa River on the Quebec side where the Ottawa meets the Schyan River there is a huge rock called Pierre Leblanc after Peter White. Peter White was a river boss for timber baron John Egan.

One time long ago at the junction of the Schyan and Ottawa Rivers, Peter White was hurrying his timbers down on the spring drive because the sooner the logs went to market, the sooner the timber barons got their money. And this one time, against his better judgment on the spring drive, Peter White sent eight of his very best men out in a pointer boat on some very rough water to loosen the key log in a log jam. They all drowned before his very eyes. He had to stand on shore and listen to their terrible cries for help and watch them all, one by one, go down forever into the deep black waters of the mighty Ottawa River.

And Peter White, a riverman who prided himself so much on his skills and his knowledge of the river, never recovered from the loss of his eight good men. He lost all his love of life and his nights became one long nightmare. He faded away and died a young man.

After his death his ghost returned to the shores of the Schyan and Ottawa Rivers to haunt the place where he lost his eight good men. And there to this day, just before a big storm blows up on the mighty Ottawa, men always hear the ghost of Peter White wailing, "Ay-aa—ay-aa, ayaa," a terrible haunting cry of grief and regret.

The Wake of Robert Conroy

MOST of the great lumbermen of the Ottawa Valley were Scottish — Gillies, McLachlin, Edwards, Gilmour, Caldwell — but three Irishmen came over on the same boat in the early 1830s, all destined to make their mark on the lumbering industry of Canada. They were Robert Conroy, John Egan, and John Foran, all of whom settled on Aylmer, Quebec as their base and there built huge stone mansions, schools, and hotels. Up river on the Ottawa itself and on its many tributaries — the Bonnechere, the Madawaska, the Black, the Dumoine — these early lumbermen built strings of shanties and stopping-places, developed huge farms in the wilderness to supply food and feed to the thousands of men employed and hundreds of horses used in their businesses.

Robert Conroy built on the Main street of Aylmer the large stone British Hotel which remains there to this day, an historic landmark. As was the business custom of the time, Conroy maintained a separate spacious and elegant apartment there for members of his family who were running the hotel. In those days the law required that either the hotel-keeper or his representative be on the premises to provide shelter and food for the weary traveler and his horses at all hours of the day or night. Someone had to be on call.

Unfortunately, Robert Conroy died young in April 1868, leaving his wife Mary to take care of the business and raise eight children. Conroy was being waked in the true Irish tradition in one of the huge drawing rooms of the British Hotel on the very night that Thomas D'Arcy McGee was assassinated in Bytown, April 7, 1868. All the people of importance in Aylmer and the surrounding district were gathered together to mourn the passing of Conroy — Symmes, Wrights, Egans, Forans, McDonalds, McCords, Shanlys, Delisles, Churches, Moores, McGooeys, McConnells, Watsons, Aylens, as well as all the relatives from Pembroke and Ironsides, Glengarry and, of course, Aylmer.

The food was bountiful, the drink flowing, the talk and storytelling endless. In those days Irish wakes lasted for three days or more non-stop with many mourners staying over and, in Conroy's case, being put up at the British.

So there was still a large crowd gathered at the British when, at two o'clock in the morning, there was a loud knocking at the heavy front doors which nobody ever used. Although they were taken aback by the knocking at the unused doors and by the lateness of the hour, the Conroy relatives answered.

It was a wild, wet, April night and a cold wind blew through the rooms as the mourners opened the doors to three cloaked men standing on the threshold holding the reins of three horses, shining with sweat and lathered in foam.

"We have come to pay our respects to Robert Conroy," one of the strange men said in a husky voice.

Although nobody could identify the men, one of Robert Conroy's sons moved forward out of the crowd and said, "Come in." He gave orders to one of the servants to take the horses to the stables and care for them. Then he offered the visitors the hospitality of the house.

The three strange men blended into the crowd, but they had aroused the curiosity of some of the mourners who noted that they constantly looked at their watches and kept getting the right time from others as though they were trying to establish very clearly the hour of their visit. They ate but little and refused all drink. They gave no one their names, stayed for an hour or so, then called for their horses and departed, leaving the mourners uneasy and full of speculations.

The next morning word came from Bytown that during the night Thomas D'Arcy McGee had been assassinated outside his boarding house. Immediately everyone thought of the three strange men who had ridden out of the wild windy night to mourn Robert Conroy. Thomas Patrick Whelan was hanged for the murder of Thomas D'Arcy McGee. But to this day there are people who claim that the three strange men who rode up to the British Hotel on the night of April 7, 1868, were really the murderers and that the wrong man was hanged in one of the very few political murders in Canadian history.

The Ghost of Long Jim Nesbitt

IT was rule in the lumber camps that, when one shantyman died or was killed or was drowned, the bosses would bring in another lad to replace him. So when Long Jim Nesbitt from Wakefield was drowned while working for Timber Baron McLaren on the Gatineau River, Billy Brennan from Brennan's Hill was hired to replace him. Naturally he was put to sleep in the empty bunk of the Long Jim Nesbitt who had been drowned in the Gatineau River. And every night in the middle of the night when Brennan was trying to sleep, the ghost of Long Jim Nesbitt would come and stand beside his bunk and pull at his bottom blanket which was spread over cedar boughs and served as a mattress.

It was really scary trying to sleep and having a ghost stand at the side of your bed and pull at your blanket.

So the first chance he got, Billy Brennan walked out from the lumber camp and went to see the priest at Farrellton.

"I am being haunted by the ghost of the dead lad who used to sleep in my bunk," he told the priest. "The ghost of Long Jim Nesbitt is haunting me and I don't know why. But it is really scary and I can't go on much longer."

So the priest told Billy Brennan what to do.

"When the ghost appears again say to him, 'In the name of God, the Father, and the Holy Ghost, what do you want of me?'"

So Billy Brennan walked back in to the camp, and sure enough, that very night, the ghost showed up again at his bedside.

Billy Brennan jumped up and said to the ghost, "In the name of God, the Father, and the Holy Ghost, what do you want of me?"

And the ghost spoke to him slowly but surely.

"Under your bottom blanket there is some money I owe to Charlie Farrell at Wakefield. I have been working all winter long to save the money to pay my debt. Will you please take the money to Charlie for me."

So Billy Brennan walked out from the lumber camp once again, all the way to Wakefield, where he paid Charlie Farrell the money he was owed by Long Jim Nesbitt.

And Nesbitt's ghost disappeared forever from the McLaren lumber camp on the Gatineau River.

The Ghost of John Sloan's Wife

JOHN Sloan was a famous bush foreman from Vinton, Quebec, who worked in the Pontiac lumber camps for years and years for Timber Baron Gillies. While he was away in the camps one winter, John Sloan's wife died. So he got permission to go down to Vinton and bury her.

But when John Sloan went back to his camp from Vinton after his wife's funeral, the teamsters kept seeing a ghost of a woman every night behind the stables when they went to put their horses in for the night. This happened night after night, scaring both men and horses. Finally, one of the teamsters got up the courage to ask her, "What the Devil do you want here?"

"I am John Sloan's wife," the ghost said. "When I died, John took my wedding ring off my finger. I want it back."

The teamsters didn't know what to do about the ghost. For a while they said nothing. But word spread through the whole camp and the men were getting very skitterish about the ghost. At last, one of the men went to Timber Baron Gillies and complained.

"The ghost of John Sloan's wife is upsetting all the men in the camp," he said. "Some of them are threatening to jump camp."

Now Timber Baron Gillies knew a disaster could occur if all his shantymen — the cutters, the hewers, the teamsters — all jumped camp. He would not get his timbers out of the bush onto the drive down the river and he would lose a fortune.

"You had better lay this ghost to rest," he said to John Sloan, "or we'll all be out of work here."

Timber Baron Gillies gave John Sloan a week off work and Sloan went back down the Ottawa Valley to Vinton. Now, the Sloans of Vinton were a very large clan and, when they heard that John Sloan intended to have his wife's body exhumed, they took sides on the issue. Some Sloans felt exhuming the body was sacrilegious, against their Roman Catholic religion, and that no good would come of such action. Others felt that the ghost must be laid to rest. They almost came to blows over it. But finally John Sloan had his wife's body exhumed. He put her wedding ring back on her finger and returned to Gillies' lumber camp.

The ghost of John Sloan's wife put in one more appearance at the stables in the Gillies' lumber camp just as the teamsters were putting the horses in for the night. She held up her ghostly left hand so all could see her golden wedding band. And then she disappeared forever from that Gillies' Lumber camp.

THIS STORY was first told to me by Gord McCullough in North Bay. Perhaps a year later I was having lunch with a friend in the Press Club in Ottawa. There I was introduced to a man named Sloan, probably in his sixties. Since I am all too well aware that the Ottawa Valley is a network of clans and that the interconnections are myriad and mysterious, I took a flying leap and said,

"And, of course, you are a Sloan from Vinton?"

"Dead on," he replied.

"And have you ever heard this story?" I asked, and told him the story of the Ghost of John Sloan's wife.

"Heard it!" he exclaimed. "I was there when they fought about whether or not the body would be exhumed."

The Devil's Forked Tail

NOT only were all the lumber camps full of ghost stories but the men were always playing tricks on one another — like putting an old sock in the stew, or a bearskin on the privy seat in the backhouse so that when the men had to go out at night they were scared to death by sitting on a bearskin, or moving all the boots under the bunks at night so that when you got up in the morning you had mismatched pairs.

Now this scary tale happened in a Booth lumber camp on the Black River. The men had just come in to the lumber camp in the late fall and it was close to freeze-up. The Booth foreman, Paddy Fitzgerald, had brought in some live cows to be slaughtered as soon as it would be cold enough to keep the meat.

Around Christmas when the cows were duly slaughtered, one of the enterprising shantymen, Wee Willie MacMillan, keen to play tricks, got one of the cowhides and shaped it so he could put it over himself like a cloak. Then he worked on the cow's tail and cleverly shaped it like the Devil's Forked Tail.

Now everyone knows that one of the ways in which the Devil always announces his coming is by the rattling of chains. Well, there was never any shortage of chains in a lumber camp, so Wee Willie got some of those.

When everything was ready, one wind-hollering moonless January night, Wee Willie put the cowhide over himself, opened the sleep camp door, and rattled his chains until he was sure everyone in the camp was wide awake. He turned around and swung the Devil's Forked Tail right into the middle of the sleep camp. And then he disappeared into the night, rattling his chains as he left.

Of course, all the men in the sleep camp were absolutely terrified, frightened out of their wits, scared to death. By next morning all the French-Canadians had fled the camp. Foreman Paddy Fitzgerald fired Wee Willie MacMillan for playing his trick. Fitzgerald had to get almost a whole new crew to replace the men who had been scared to death, and the Booth Lumber Company had to spend months chasing down all the men who had jumped camp.

But it didn't matter at all. Shantymen in that lumber camp still kept hearing the Devil rattle his chains. And kept seeing the Devil enter and swing his forked tail. And men kept jumping camp so much that finally Timber Baron Booth had to burn down his lumber camp on the Black River in order to get rid of the Devil and his forked tail.

The Return of the Dead

IN bygone days playing weird pranks on superstitious French-Canadian shantymen was a common practice among their less credulous Protestant English-speaking associates in the lumber camps of the Ottawa Valley. In an *Ottawa Citizen* of the 1930s, Edward C. Wright, one of the many relatives of founding father Philemon Wright of Hull, Quebec, told this story about his father, E.V. Wright, and a sensational trick he played, which truly spooked those involved.

When Wright was absent from one of his lumber camps north of old Fort Temiscaming, a crew of his men, while "banking" the shanty, unearthed an Indian grave containing not only the bones of the departed brave, but also a few trinkets, the head of an axe, and a bronze pot. The pot, when opened, was found to contain a series of measures similar to those used for medicinal purposes in the old-time apothecary. The clamp on the lid of the pot was in the shape of a snake. These findings led the men to believe they had opened the grave of a Native witch doctor and not a common brave.

When Wright returned to the camp a few days later he was informed of the discovery and the kind of uneasiness it was beginning to cause in his camp among the men. He ordered the bones removed to the storehouse back of the shanty. The following day he instructed one of his French-Canadian shantymen to go to the storehouse and fetch a bag of flour. The man dutifully started out on his errand but returned to Wright a few moments later explaining he was afraid to go into the storehouse while the bones were there.

This open display of fear gave one of the English-speaking shantymen a sinister idea. He said to Wright, "Let's pretend that you are a Freemason and that all Freemasons are gifted with the power to raise the dead. We can have some fun."

Well, lumberman Wright, always ready for a lark, fell in with the dark plot. So that evening, Wright, with some of his men, set the stage for a hair-raising drama. Rotten wood was piled on to the camboose fire to make plenty of smoke. A dummy was rigged up in

Native garments and placed on the roof of the shanty with a rope attached to it. When darkness set in and all the shantymen — except two or three who had to be on the roof — were sitting around the fire, someone started a conversation about the finding of the bones.

"Is it true, Mr. Wright," one of the shantymen asked, "that you can bring the dead back to life?"

"Oh, yes," Wright said. "I possess that power from my ancestors."

"Well, then, can you bring the dead Indian back to life?"

"Oh, yes, indeed," Wright said. "I can demonstrate it right here and now."

While the entire camp looked on in wonder and horror, Wright rose from his place, stood before the camboose fire, made a few mystic signs with his hands, and called out, "Oh, spirit of the disinterred Indian, leave now your happy hunting ground and return to us here on earth."

Well, this wild incantation alone had the effect of striking fear into the hearts of some of the men. But when a moment later there was a great commotion on the roof of the shanty and the dummy figure of the Native came hurtling down into the flames, there was the wildest disorder as the men fled in all directions. Some dropped to their knees to say "Holy Marys." Some jumped into their bunks and hid under the blankets.

Meantime, the three men on the roof hauled the dummy up through the chimney hole again. Then, as had been arranged to heighten the terror among the superstitious, they rushed into the shanty, tearing at their hair and crying out, "We have just seen an Indian come through the roof. We have just seen an Indian come through the roof and fly heavenward in a sheet of flame!"

At this point, truly terrified at this return from the dead, a good number of Wrights's men fled into the woods.

In actual fact Wright paid for his sensational trick. The most terrified of the men left camp, never to return. And it took him days to quiet down some of the others who remained.

The Body
in the Oats Bin

NOW, in the early days in the Ottawa Valley in all the lumber camps there were shantymen of every race and creed and tongue — Polish, Scottish, German, English, Irish, French, Indian, Swedish. But they all spoke English — of one kind or another.

In the wintertime way back in the bush, shantymen would sometimes be killed by a falling tree or bleed to death from an axe wound or die from the flu. And there would be no way to get the body out to a funeral parlor or even to their homes for burial. So they used to put the dead bodies in the oats bin, because if you leave a body out when it's cold, it blackens, but if you pack it in oats, it doesn't.

Many of the shantymen were superstitious and easily scared way back in the bush miles and miles from anyone or anywhere. But the French-Canadians were perhaps the most superstitious of all. And one time away back in a McLaren lumber camp on the Lièvre River, this poor lad died of pneumonia. There was no way to get the body out, so they put it in the oats bin in the stables.

Now, it used to be a rule in the lumber camp that the last shantyman to eat his evening meal did the stable chores and the last check on all the teams of indispensable horses. So one night it was this French-Canadian lad's turn to do the chores. And the other shantymen in the camp thought they'd have some fun with him, play a trick. They propped the dead body up in the oats bin and put a hat on him. Then they all got themselves lined up at the sleep camp window — there was only one — to watch the fun.

The French-Canadian lad's sleigh came in with its lantern hung on the sleigh-post. They watched it swinging and swaying. Then they watched the lad unharness his horses, unhook the lantern, and put them into the stable. And then they saw the lantern moving real slow across the yard towards the granary where the oats were stored. They saw him open up the granary door and they watched the lantern light go in.

Then all of a sudden they heard a terrible cry and they watched the French-Canadian lad go like crazy, the lantern swinging madly back and forth, as he took off into the bush and disappeared from the camp!

The shantymen from the camp searched for him for three days, but he was never found. And it has always been said he was eaten by the Wendigo.

The Devil Meets Big Joe Dufour

NOW, we already know, of course, that in the early days of lumbering the Devil spent considerable time on earth in the Ottawa Valley. That was how he had his honeymoon on the Ottawa River where he changed his bride to stone and started the Devil's Garden from his left-over onion sandwiches.

This scary story happened about the time that Giant Joe Montferrand was King of the Ottawa River and Giant Paul Bunyan had left Canada and gone to the United States. But this story is about another lumbering giant, Big Joe Dufour from Three Rivers, Quebec, who used to work in the lumber camps for timber baron Conroy at Amable du Fond on the Eau Claire River.

Now, Joe Dufour was big and tough and strong and tall like all the other river bosses. But he wasn't like them in one way. The other river bosses and shantymen loved to talk, and sing and dance, and play tricks on each other, and be together. But Big Joe Dufour used to go by himself all the time.

And the other river bosses and shantymen used to say to him, "You should not go alone so much in the bush, Joe Dufour. Someday you will meet the Devil." But Big Joe Dufour paid no attention to them.

Then one time he was walking through the bush from Mattawa to his lumber camp at Amable du Fond. Suddenly a voice roared to him out of the trees and the dark forest.

"Who goes there?"

"Big Joe Dufour goes here," thundered back Dufour.

"Big Joe Dufour pass by," said the voice out of the trees and the dark forest.

"Who dares to tell Big Joe Dufour to pass by?" demanded Big Joe.

"Big Joe Dufour pass by," the voice replied from the trees and the dark forest. "But Big Joe Dufour go small like that."

And Big Joe Dufour lost his height and his strength, and became a little man, useless

And Big Joe Dufour lost his height and his strength, and became a little man, useless as Samson, because Big Joe Dufour, always traveling alone, had finally met the Devil.

The Horse-Fish

ONE time long ago in the lumbering days of the Ottawa Valley, a shantyman from Chapeau was crossing the ice where the waters of the Dumoine River and the Ottawa River blend together. He was crossing over with a favorite horse and sleigh when suddenly he hit an ice bubble. The ice cracked and the water opened, swallowing up the shantyman's horse and sleigh. The shantyman from Chapeau rescued himself by jumping free, but he had to walk twenty miles in to the nearest McLachlin lumber camp where he was fed and warmed by the woodstove.

Now, the shantyman from Chapeau missed his favorite horse very much. So the following spring, curious about what might be left around the scene of his accident, he returned to the junction of the Dumoine and Ottawa Rivers to the very spot where he had lost his horse and sleigh. There he looked down into the clear fresh waters.

At first he saw only his own reflection. He bent over and peered deeper into the water. And then, to his amazement, he beheld below him an enormous horse-fish swimming along through the waters complete in his favorite horse's harness, with the reins trailing out behind him!

Over the years since then many travelers, canoeists, and fishermen have reported seeing the horse-fish in the water at the very spot where the old shantyman hit the ice bubble. Great fishermen from all over Canada, indeed from all over the world, have been guided to the spot by fishing guides who have seen the great horse-fish. But so far all that has happened is that their expensive tackle has been caught in the harness and lost, and a couple of stubborn fishermen who refused to let go of their lines have been pulled into the river and drowned.

Now, if you are lucky enough to look down into the water there and catch a glimpse of the great horse-fish you will see the ghostly figures of the drowned fishermen, still holding on to their tackle and trailing along behind!

The Burial of Bandy Burke

NE time in a Gillies lumber camp on the Pickanock River a shantyman named Bandy Burke died on the job. It was the middle of January, so, as was the custom in the lumber camps in the wintertime when such things occurred, the body of Bandy Burke was put in the oats bin where it would be kept frozen until burial some time in the spring when the ground thawed out enough to dig six feet down.

But two of Bandy's old friends, Jacques and Joe Gervais, as good Roman Catholics were upset and concerned about Bandy not having a proper Christian burial and being so long delayed in purgatory in the oats bin. Besides, they also knew that Bandy's family would want his body returned to be waked and buried in his home-place. So they went to the Gillies foreman and volunteered to walk the body out of the lumber camp to the undertaker at Fort Coulonge for family and priestly ministrations there. Jacques and Joe made a good argument for the long trip and, surprisingly, the Gillies foreman gave them permission.

"But be back in four days," he said, "or you'll both be fired."

Jacques and Joe started out on the forty-mile hike in the twenty-five below degrees temperatures with the frozen "stiff" on their shoulders wrapped still in the clothes in which he had died. Even Bandy's hand-knit toque was still frozen to his hair.

Jacques and Joe hadn't gone very far on the narrow tote-road when they realized they had a problem on their hands. Jacques was a little wee Frenchman who took after his mother's side of the family. Joe was six-foot-three like his father. Because of the big difference in their height, Bandy's body kept sliding off Joe's shoulders, down past Jacques, and into the snow. They tried it different ways. If Jacques went first and Joe went second, then the body slid forwards into the snow. If Joe went first and Jacques went second, the body slid backwards into the snow.

"Well, Bandy," said Jacques to his frozen stiff friend, "At this rate we'll not get you home until you've melted in the spring."

"Yes," said Joe, "I'd say we're losing ground all the time."

They kept walking ahead on the narrow tote-road. But if Jacques went first and Joe went second, then the body slid forwards into the snow. If Joe went first and Jacques went second, the body slid backwards into the snow.

"At this rate we'll never make it back in four days," Joe said.

"Yes, we have to do something," Jacques said.

They kept walking ahead on the narrow tote-road. But if Jacques went first and Joe went second, then the body slid forward into the snow. If Joe went first and Jacques went second, the body slid backwards into the snow.

Finally, they came to a trapper's halfway cabin where they were going to bed down for the night. The trappers' halfway cabins always had emergency supplies like a can of frozen beans, an axe, a bucksaw, and a sawhorse, all for getting wood ready for a fire.

Jacques and Joe looked at each other.

"I have an idea," said Jacques.

"I have the same idea," said Joe.

The two friends reverently placed the body of Bandy Burke on the sawhorse, took the bucksaw off the wall and sawed the frozen corpse in half.

The next morning, each easily carrying half of the body strapped on his back, Joe and Jacques hit the tote-road trail again, making very good time to the undertaker's in Fort Coulonge where the two pieces of Bandy Burke were put together again and prepared for proper wake and burial.